Dear Parent:
Your child's love of reading starts here!

Every child learns to read in a different way and at his or her own speed. Some go back and forth between reading levels and read favorite books again and again. Others read through each level in order. You can help your young reader improve and become more confident by encouraging his or her own interests and abilities. From books your child reads with you to the first books he or she reads alone, there are I Can Read Books for every stage of reading:

SHARED READING
Basic language, word repetition, and whimsical illustrations, ideal for sharing with your emergent reader

BEGINNING READING
Short sentences, familiar words, and simple concepts for children eager to read on their own

READING WITH HELP
Engaging stories, longer sentences, and language play for developing readers

READING ALONE
Complex plots, challenging vocabulary, and high-interest topics for the independent reader

I Can Read Books have introduced children to the joy of reading since 1957. Featuring award-winning authors and illustrators and a fabulous cast of beloved characters, I Can Read Books set the standard for beginning readers.

A lifetime of discovery begins with the magical words **"I Can Read!"**

Visit www.icanread.com for information
on enriching your child's reading experience.

Pinkalicious
Kindergarten Fun

To Florence
—V.K.

The author gratefully acknowledges
the artistic and editorial contributions of
Daniel Griffo and Jacqueline Resnick.

I Can Read® and I Can Read Book® are trademarks of HarperCollins Publishers.

Pinkalicious: Kindergarten Fun
Copyright © 2022 by VBK, Co.

PINKALICIOUS and all related logos and characters are trademarks of VBK, Co. Used with permission.

Based on the HarperCollins book *Pinkalicious* written by
Victoria Kann and Elizabeth Kann, illustrated by Victoria Kann
For information address HarperCollins Children's Books, a division of HarperCollins Publishers,
195 Broadway, New York, NY 10007.
www.icanread.com

Library of Congress Control Number: 2021950861
ISBN 978-0-06-300385-9 (hardcover)—ISBN 978-0-06-300384-2 (pbk.)

22 23 24 25 26 LSCC 10 9 8 7 6 5 4 3 2 1
❖
First Edition

Pinkalicious
Kindergarten Fun

by Victoria Kann

HARPER
An Imprint of HarperCollinsPublishers

My class was getting
kindergarten buddies!
We were going to spend
the whole day with them.

"Pinkalicious, meet Mia,"
said Ms. Diaz,
the kindergarten teacher.
"We're going to have
so much fun," I said to Mia.

"Hula-hooping is fun.

Baking cupcakes is fun.

Kindergarten is NOT fun,"

Mia said.

I couldn't believe my ears.

"Kindergarten is pinkatastically,
pinkamazingly fun!"
I said to Mia.

"I'll show you all the fun
things to do in kindergarten,"
I promised.

"I have big news,"

Ms. Diaz told my class.

"Today YOU get to be the teacher

for your kindergarten buddy!"

"Pinkawow," I said.

"I've always wanted

to be a teacher!"

"We'll start with math,"
said Ms. Diaz.

"Math is fun!" I said to Mia.

"Let me show you why."

I got my lunch box.

"What is one cupcake

plus one cupcake?" I asked.

"Two cupcakes," said Mia.

"Let's subtract cupcakes," I said.

"How do we do that?" Mia asked.

"We eat them!" I said.

"Math is yummy," Mia said.

"It's yumtastic!" I agreed.

"You have just enough time to dress up as your favorite book characters before story time!" Ms. Diaz said.

"I love dressing up!" said Mia.

"Can we join you?" asked Molly.

"That sounds fun!" said Florence,
Molly's buddy.

"Story time!" I said.

"What book did everyone pick?"

"We all chose lots of fairy tales,"
Florence said proudly.

"This one is my favorite,"
said Mia.

"Mine too," Molly said.

I began to read.

"Once upon a pinkness . . ."

Ms. Diaz took us to recess next.

I had to show Mia

that recess was fun!

"Let's hula-hoop," I said.

"Watch what I can do," Mia said.

She spun the hoop on her leg.

"Go, Mia!" Florence said.

"That was hulamazing," I said.

"It's writing time,"
Ms. Diaz said after recess.
"You can write anything you want."
"I know!" I said.
"Let's write notes to each other!"
"Okay!" said Mia.

For science time,

Ms. Diaz gave us

supplies to make slime.

"This is going to be fun," I said.

I poured, and Mia mixed.

"My slime is ooey gooey!"
Mia said.

"Mine is icky sticky!" Florence said.

"They're both slimetastic!" I said.

Our next subject was art.
"I'm going to make the
pinkest painting!" Mia said.

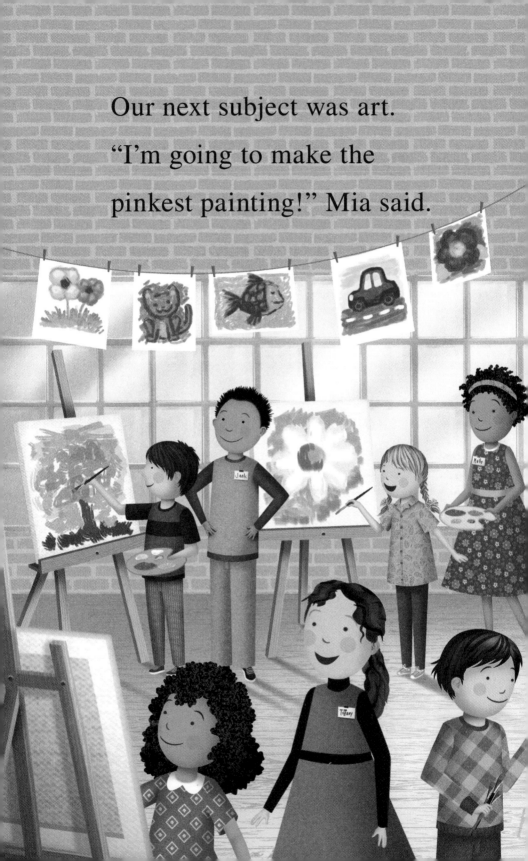

"Oh no!" Mia gasped.

"I got blue paint

on my perfectly pink painting!"

"I know what to do," I said.

"You can add more colors!"

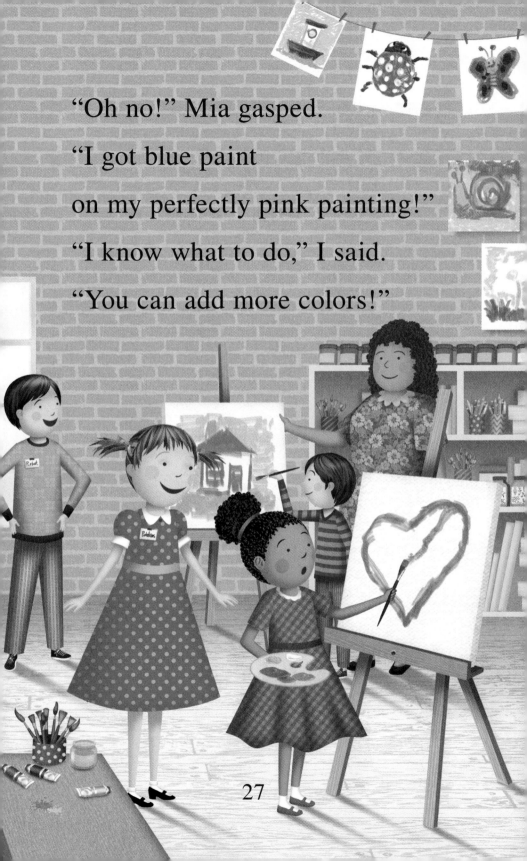

"I can help you, Mia," Florence said.

"Me too," said Molly.

"Me three," I said.

We got more paint for Mia.

"Thanks," Mia said.

"I feel better now."

"Wow," I said.

"Your painting is colorrific!"

"It's for you," Mia said.

"It's a heart for my new friend."

"I love it!" I said.

I gave Mia a hug.

"You never answered my note,"
I said.

"Do you think kindergarten

is fun?"

"It's not just fun," Mia said.

"It's FUNTASTIC!"

We all laughed.

"What is the best part?" I asked.

"I love learning new things
and making new friends!"
Mia cheered.